TRON LEGACY
THE MOVIE STORYBOOK

Written by James Ponti
Based on the screenplay written by Eddy Kitsis & Adam Horowitz
Based on characters created by Steven Lisberger and Bonnie MacBird
Executive Producer Donald Kushner
Produced by Sean Bailey, Jeffrey Silver, Steven Lisberger
Directed by Joseph Kosinski

Printed in the United States of America

First edition

1 3 5 7 9 10 6 8 4 2

V381-8386-5-10244

Library of Congress Catalog Card Number on file

ISBN 978-1-4231-3157-1

SUSTAINABLE FORESTRY INITIATIVE

Certified Chain of Custody
35% Certified Forests,
65% Certified Fiber Sourcing
www.sfiprogram.org

Disney PRESS New York

D1372896

Most parents told bedtime stories that took place in faraway kingdoms with brave knights and clever princesses. But Kevin Flynn wasn't like most parents. He was a computer genius who designed some of the world's most famous video games. At night, he told his son Sam tales of a cyber world known as the Grid, where digital warriors battled against evil.

The hero of those stories was named Tron. Tron wasn't just in Kevin's stories. He was also the star of Kevin's most famous video game.

What Sam had no way of knowing was that the Grid was a world Kevin had created!

"Don't go into work tonight," Sam said one night as Kevin prepared to leave.

"How about tomorrow we hit the arcade?" Kevin said with a smile. "Maybe you can take a crack at your old man's high score."

Sam watched through the bedroom window as his father climbed onto his motorcycle and rode off into the darkness.

He never came back.

The disappearance of Kevin Flynn was a total mystery. Twenty years later, Sam was visited by an old family friend.

Sam returned home one night and found Alan Bradley waiting for him. Alan had been his father's business partner and had tried to keep an eye out on Sam.

"Why are you in my apartment?" Sam asked, surprised.

"I promised you if I ever got any information about your dad, I'd tell you first," Alan said as he reached into his pocket and pulled out an old-style pager. Before cell phones, pagers were used to contact people.

"I was paged last night," he said. "The page came from the arcade."

That didn't make any sense. Flynn's arcade was once one of the most popular places in town. But now it was just an old abandoned building.

"These are the keys to the arcade," Alan said. "I haven't gone over there yet. I thought you should be the one."

Sam didn't know how to respond. "You're acting like I'm going to find him sitting there working," he joked.

Alan didn't laugh. "Wouldn't that be something?"

That night, Sam rode his motorcycle to the abandoned arcade. He smiled when he looked down the center row and saw his favorite game of all—Tron.

Out of habit, he reached into his pocket and pulled out a quarter. He smiled as he thought about playing one more time. He dropped the quarter in the slot, but the game didn't turn on. Instead, the quarter clattered down through the coin-return chute and onto the floor.

When Sam kneeled down to pick it up, he noticed the floor. It had been scuffed by someone repeatedly moving the game back and forth. He reached around the side of the machine and gave it a yank. The game moved, revealing an opening in the wall.

Sam headed downstairs and discovered his father's old office and lab!

Sam touched the computer's screen, and, much to his surprise, it came to life. A question appeared on the screen. TRON PROJECT—INITIATE SEQUENCE?

Sam shrugged and thought, *Why not?* He typed Y for yes. Without warning, a burning blue flash filled the room.

For a moment, Sam was blinded. When his vision cleared, he shrugged. His father wasn't here. He went back upstairs.

When Sam finally got outside, the street looked *different*. There was a blue haze everywhere, and a fog hung over the city. Sam looked for his motorcycle, but it had vanished.

Suddenly another blinding light shone down on him. At first, he thought it was a helicopter. But when he looked up in the sky, he realized it was something very different. The aircraft looked exactly like the one from his Tron toys. It was shaped like an upside-down U and was called a Recognizer.

A voice boomed from above: "Identify yourself, program!"

As the ship landed, a door opened to reveal two Sentries. This was when Sam realized that he was not on the street outside the arcade. He was inside his father's computer!

This was the Grid, and it was REAL.

"This program has no disc," one Sentry announced as they approached. "Another stray."

"Wait! Wait!" Sam yelped desperately as they pulled him onto the ship. From his father's stories, he knew that although the others looked like people, they were actually computer programs. All programs on the Grid had discs that carried their memory and source code. He tried to explain that the reason he didn't have a disc was that he wasn't a program. The Sentries didn't listen and pushed him along.

The Recognizer docked, and Sam was put into a long line of "strays." At the front of the line, a Sentry assigned destinations for each new arrival. "I know you probably get this a lot," Sam pleaded with the guard. "But there's been a mistake. I need to talk to somebody."

The Sentry ignored him and announced his verdict: "Games."

Before Sam knew what was going on, he was taken to an armory where a group of female programs called Sirens outfitted him in body armor—just like the kind Tron wore during his battles in the video game.

The games reminded Sam of the video games he played with his father. But there was no off switch here. This was apparent when Sam saw a competitor lose a match and scatter into a million pixels. They had been derezzed.

When he stepped into the stadium, Sam felt as if he was in a futuristic coliseum. A large crowd was waiting for the games to begin.

When a program threw his disc, it turned into a weapon and would always return. Sam stepped in for the first battle.

High above the arena, a helmeted figure looked down on the crowd. He was in charge of the Grid, and he was responsible for the dangerous game that was about to begin.

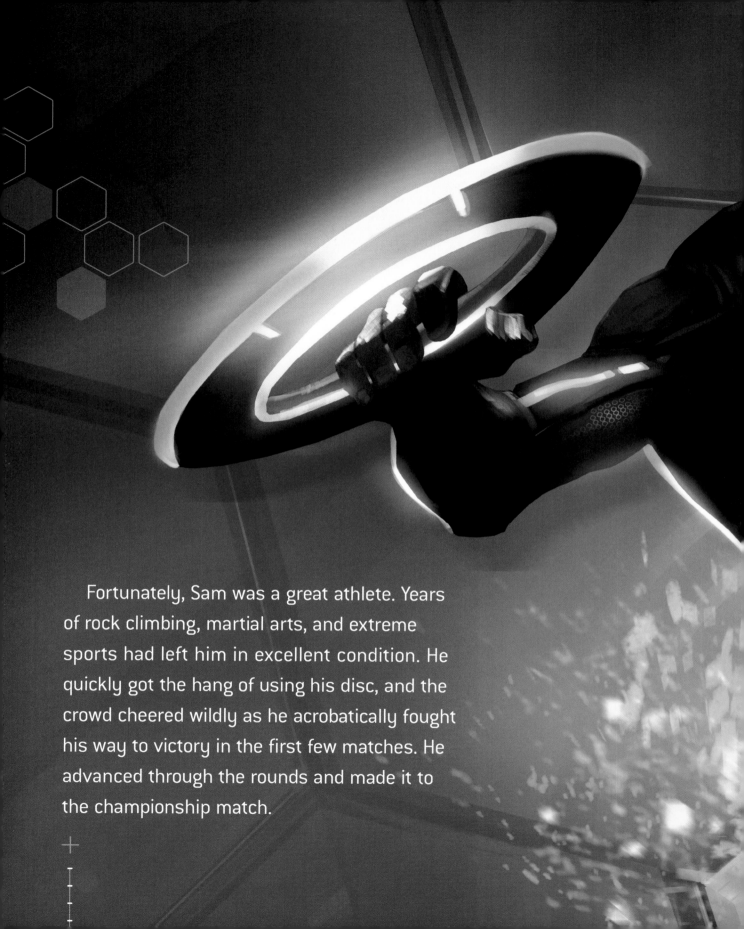

Fortunately, Sam was a great athlete. Years of rock climbing, martial arts, and extreme sports had left him in excellent condition. He quickly got the hang of using his disc, and the crowd cheered wildly as he acrobatically fought his way to victory in the first few matches. He advanced through the rounds and made it to the championship match.

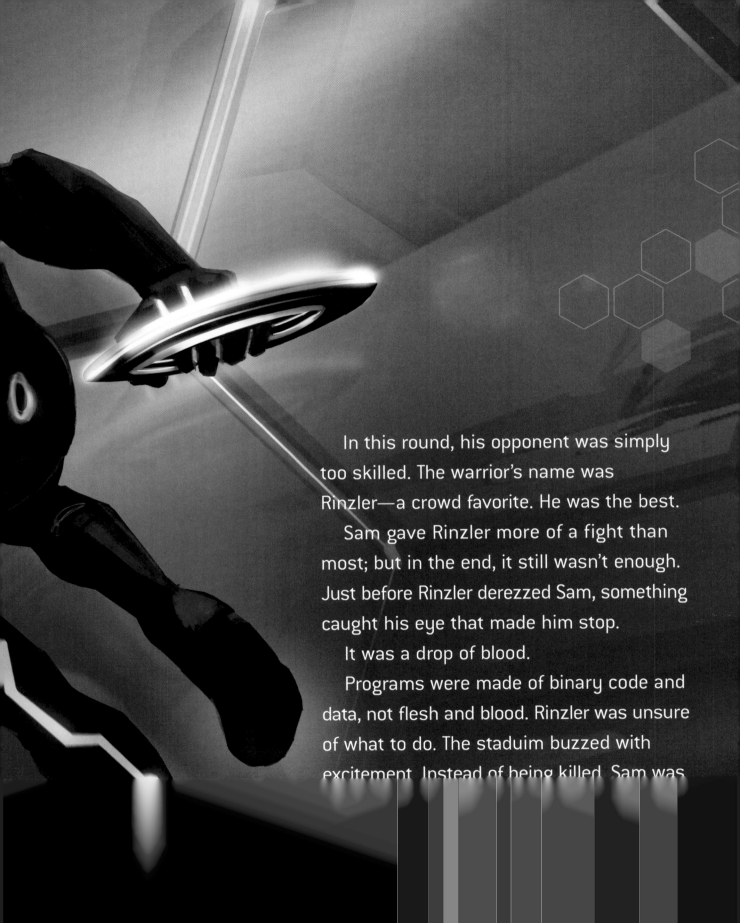

In this round, his opponent was simply too skilled. The warrior's name was Rinzler—a crowd favorite. He was the best.

Sam gave Rinzler more of a fight than most; but in the end, it still wasn't enough. Just before Rinzler derezzed Sam, something caught his eye that made him stop.

It was a drop of blood.

Programs were made of binary code and data, not flesh and blood. Rinzler was unsure of what to do. The staduim buzzed with excitement. Instead of being killed, Sam was

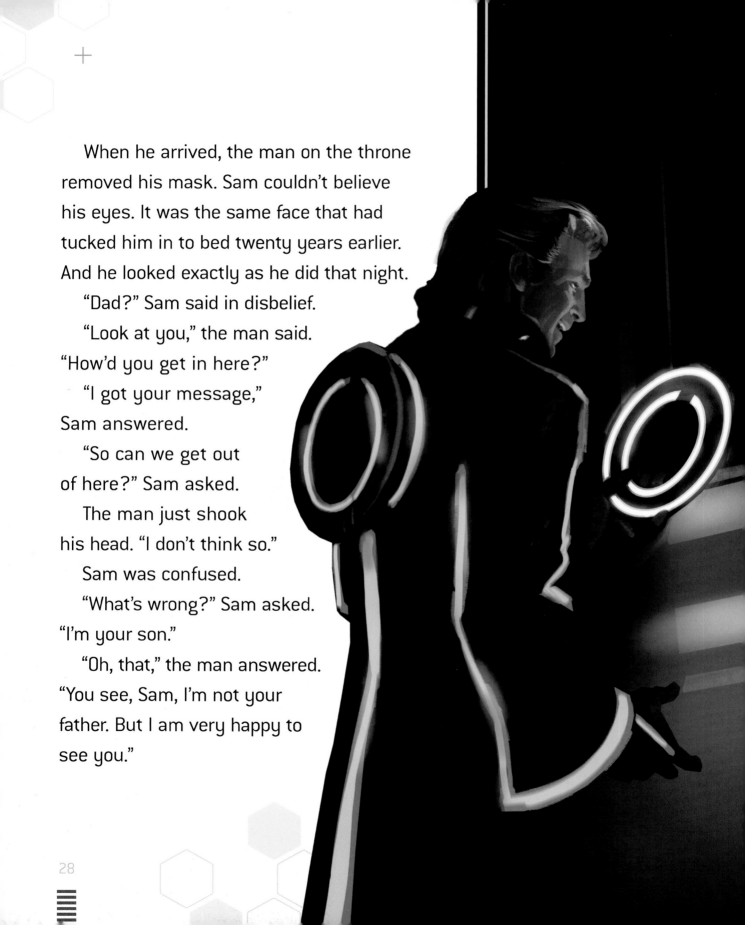

When he arrived, the man on the throne removed his mask. Sam couldn't believe his eyes. It was the same face that had tucked him in to bed twenty years earlier. And he looked exactly as he did that night.

"Dad?" Sam said in disbelief.

"Look at you," the man said. "How'd you get in here?"

"I got your message," Sam answered.

"So can we get out of here?" Sam asked.

The man just shook his head. "I don't think so."

Sam was confused.

"What's wrong?" Sam asked. "I'm your son."

"Oh, that," the man answered. "You see, Sam, I'm not your father. But I am very happy to see you."

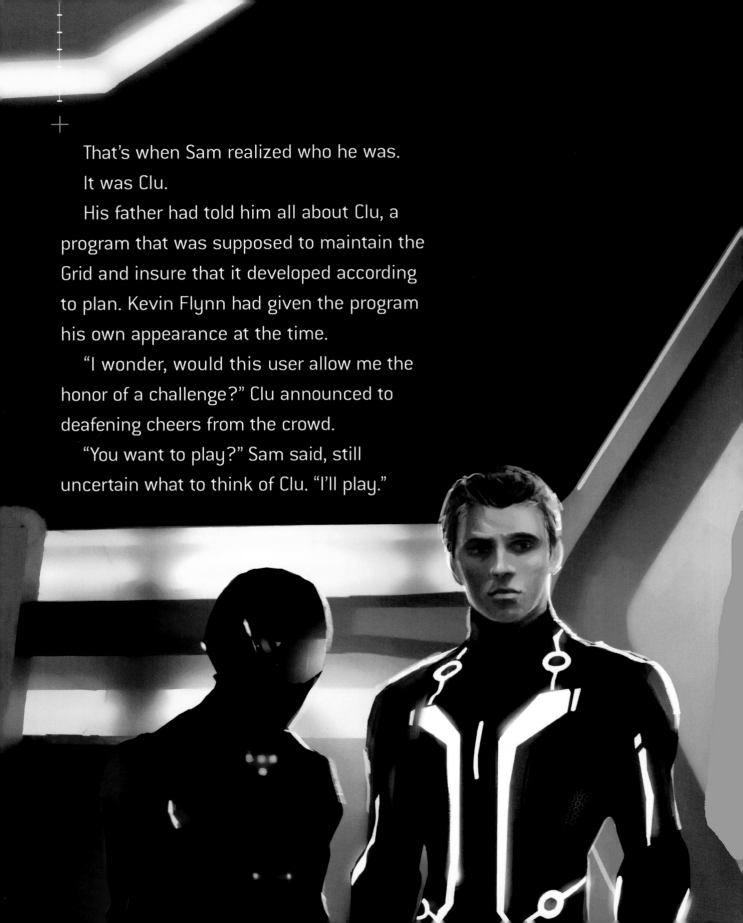

That's when Sam realized who he was. It was Clu.

His father had told him all about Clu, a program that was supposed to maintain the Grid and insure that it developed according to plan. Kevin Flynn had given the program his own appearance at the time.

"I wonder, would this user allow me the honor of a challenge?" Clu announced to deafening cheers from the crowd.

"You want to play?" Sam said, still uncertain what to think of Clu. "I'll play."

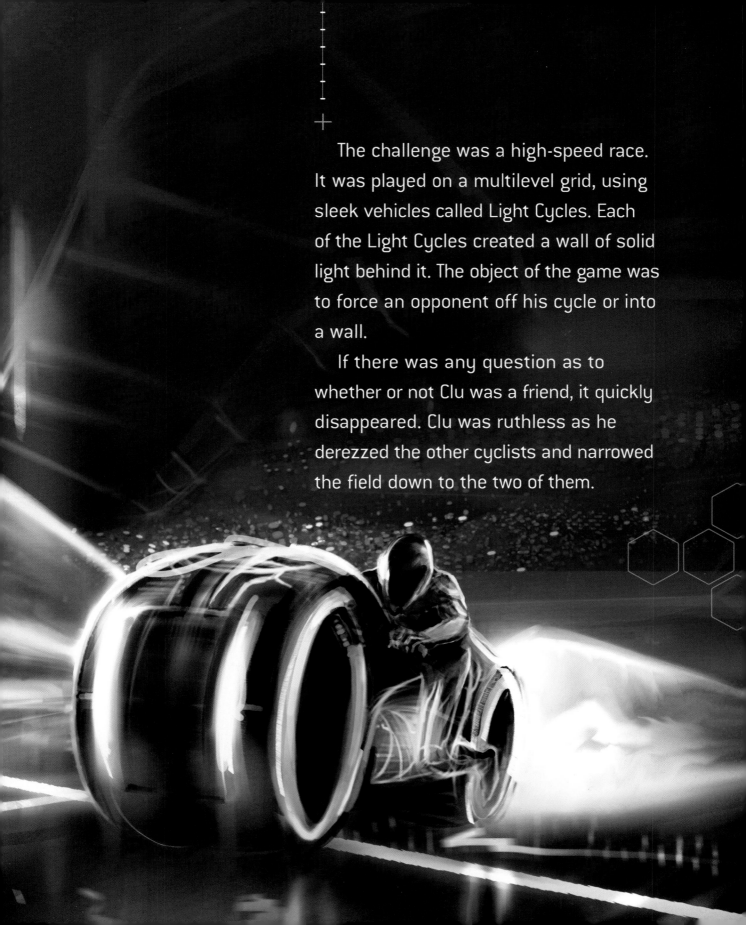

The challenge was a high-speed race. It was played on a multilevel grid, using sleek vehicles called Light Cycles. Each of the Light Cycles created a wall of solid light behind it. The object of the game was to force an opponent off his cycle or into a wall.

If there was any question as to whether or not Clu was a friend, it quickly disappeared. Clu was ruthless as he derezzed the other cyclists and narrowed the field down to the two of them.

Sam was good, but Clu had experience on his side. He rammed Sam and knocked him off his Light Cycle. Then he looped around to finish him off. Rather than run and hide, Sam stood his ground. This act of bravery brought huge cheers from the crowd.

Just before Clu reached him, another vehicle made a surprise entrance. It was a sleek four-wheeled car that raced across the battle grid. The Light Runner made a wall to protect Sam and then came to a screeching halt.

The top flipped open to reveal a masked driver, who yelled, "Get in!"

Sam quickly dove into the Light Runner, which sped off.

Sam turned to find some of Clu's men still chasing them. The driver gunned the engine and headed straight for the boundary wall that marked the edge of the gaming arena.

Just when it looked as if they were about to slam into the wall, the driver flipped a switch, firing two missiles creating a hole in the wall. The vehicle drove through and continued into the darkness.

The mask on the driver's helmet slid open to reveal a beautiful woman with short black hair.

"I'm Quorra," she said to Sam.

Sam looked back and saw that the Light Cycles had stopped at the hole in the arena's wall.

"They're turning around!" he said gleefully.

"Not by choice," she explained. "They can't go off the Grid. They'll lose power."

"Where are you taking me?"

Quorra smiled as she drove on. "Patience, Sam Flynn. All your questions will soon be answered."

After getting far away from the city, they reached a mountain range.

They drove through a secret entrance, and Quorra took Sam to a dark room that had a magnificent view of the landscape. In the middle of the room a man sat in deep meditation.

"We have a guest," Quorra said.

"There are no guests, Quorra," the man said as he gracefully got to his feet. When he did, he stopped and smiled in disbelief.

"Sam?"

Sam knew for certain that this was no computer program.

Kevin Flynn was alive.

That night, father and son had dinner together for the first time in a very long time. Flynn tried to explain why he hadn't returned all those years ago.

He told Sam that the system was designed so that the only way in or out was through a portal, which only appeared when someone entered the Grid. "I tried to come home," he said sadly. "But the Portal closed on me."

"So we can go now," Sam answered with a smile. "We can make a run for it. Get you out of here."

Flynn just shook his head.

"What?" Sam demanded. "What is it?"

Quorra explained that if Flynn stepped foot on the Grid, Clu would be able to stop them. Clu desperately wanted the disc that contained Flynn's memory and knowledge of the Grid.

"My disc is the way out. And not just for me," Flynn tried to explain.

All three of them knew that Clu's evil manner would be incredibly dangerous in the "real" world.

"So that's it?" Sam said angrily. "We just do nothing? We just sit here?"

Sam was frustrated beyond belief. That night he talked to Quorra.

"There's someone I once knew," she said. "A program named Zuse. I haven't seen him in a long time, but they say he can get anyone anywhere."

"How do I find him?" Sam asked.

Quorra gave him a card with a small map of the Grid. "This is his sector," she said, pointing to it. "Make it there alive, and he'll find you."

Late that night, Sam rode back toward the city on his father's Light Cycle.

In the city he saw a familiar face. It was one of the Sirens who had outfitted him before entering the disc games.

"I can help you, Sam Flynn," she said. "I know who you're looking for."

She led him to the End of Line Club, the ultimate nightclub on the Grid.

Sam knew he had to find Zuse, but Zuse ended up finding Sam first.

"I need to get to the Portal," Sam told him.

"It's quite the journey," Zuse answered. "Beyond the far reaches of the Outlands and over the Sea of Simulation."

"You can help me?" Sam asked.

"Of course."

Just as Sam was beginning to feel relieved, four of Clu's Black Guard crashed through the skylight above them. Sam realized that Zuse had betrayed him. He was working for Clu.

"The game has changed, Son of Flynn," Zuse told him.

One of the guards threw his disc at Sam.
Just as it was about to hit him, another disc
came from behind and knocked it away.

Sam turned to see who had just saved him.
It was Quorra—she saved his life again!

The two of them joined forces and battled
the guards.

They were almost to the exit when one of
the Black Guard injured Quorra. Sam tried to

Suddenly, a hooded figure appeared and sent a surge of energy crackling through the club.

Kevin Flynn had returned.

"Stay with me," he instructed Sam. They used the confusion to pull Quorra to safety and managed to make it to an elevator. But as the door was shutting, one of the guards managed to grab the disc from Flynn's back.

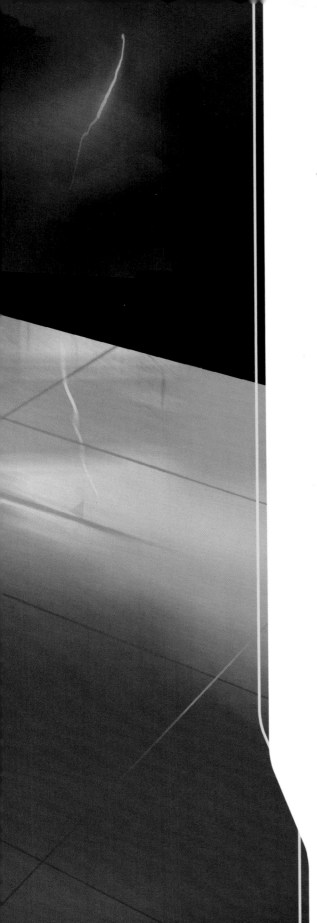

They escaped into the sublevels beneath the city and slipped aboard a cargo ship.

The ship left the dock and glided along a beam of light. As they headed toward the Portal, Flynn looked down at the injured Quorra and began trying to heal her.

"Is she going to make it?" Sam asked.

"I don't know," Flynn answered. "I have to identify the damaged code. It's enormously complex."

"She risked herself for me," Sam said sadly.

Flynn smiled at his son. "Some things are worth the risk."

He went back to work and identified the damaged code on her disc. A colored neon braid began to form; it healed her wounds.

"Now that's impressive, if I do say so myself," Flynn announced.

Later, when Quorra woke up, Sam told her where they were.

"Clu has the disc?" she asked.

Sam nodded. "Don't worry. Once I get out, I can shut him down."

Flynn saw something that worried him. It was a giant ship, nearly a mile long, called a Rectifier. Their ship suddenly changed course.

"What happened?" Sam asked.

"A new course," Flynn said ominously.

They looked out and saw that their ship was being drawn into Clu's ship. It was packed with inactive programs.

"What's this?" Quorra asked.

"Clu can't create programs," Flynn explained. "He can only destroy or repurpose."

Quorra was confused. "Repurpose for what?"

Now they could see that the Rectifier was a massive military base. They saw numerous vehicles being unloaded from some of the other ships, and there were thousands of programs in military formations.

"He's building an army," Sam said.

Just then, they saw Rinzler and the Black Guard. Quorra realized they needed a distraction to escape.

She handed her disc to Flynn and said, "Good-bye."

"Wait!" he said.

It was too late. Quorra bolted down the aisle between the containers, making sure to capture the attention of Rinzler.

Sam couldn't believe it. Once again, she was sacrificing her safety for his. "We can't just let her go!"

"We have no other choice," Flynn said.

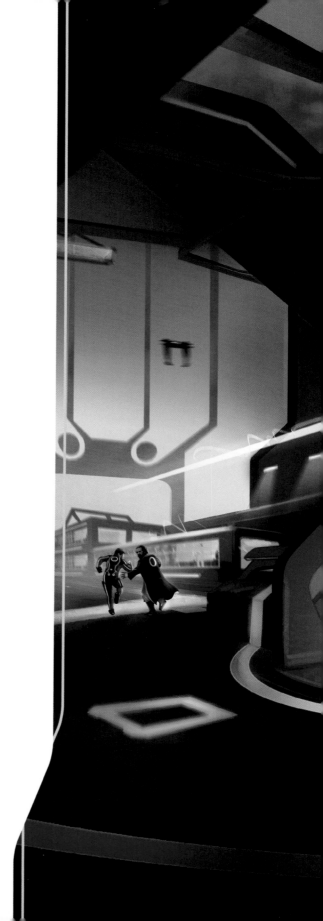

The guards quickly grabbed Quorra.

Father and son looked for a way off the ship. On the bridge of the ship, they found a special case that held Flynn's glowing disc.

"Your disc!" Sam exclaimed. "We have to get it!"

"No," Flynn said. "We beat him to the Portal. You can shut him down. From the outside."

"What about Quorra?" Sam asked, knowing they had to save her. "Some things are worth the risk."

When he reached the bridge, he found both the disc and Quorra. She was being guarded by Rinzler, the champion who beat Sam in the disc game.

Sam quickly threw his disc, and Rinzler blocked it. Then, in a flash, Sam threw his father's disc. Rinzler was stunned, and Quorra kicked him off of the platform.

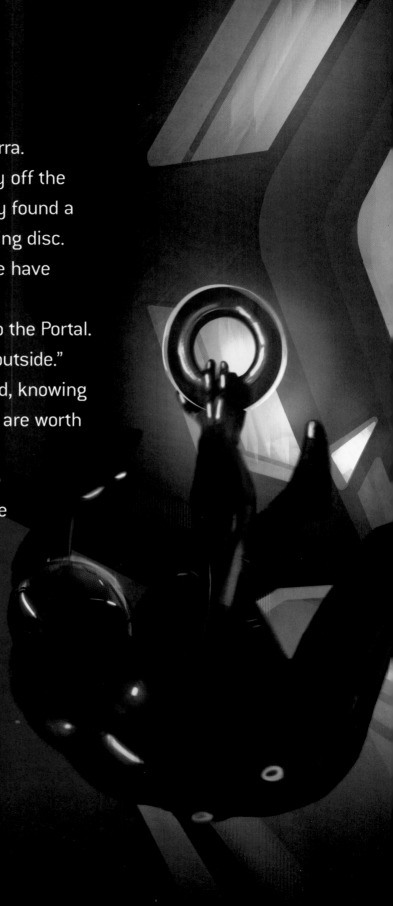

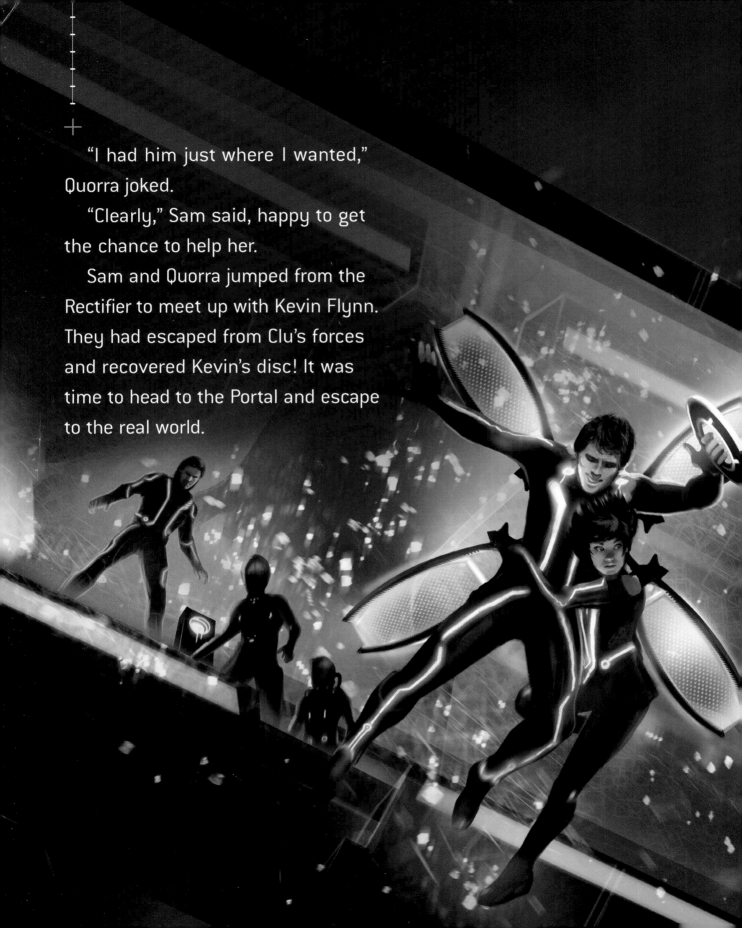

"I had him just where I wanted," Quorra joked.

"Clearly," Sam said, happy to get the chance to help her.

Sam and Quorra jumped from the Rectifier to meet up with Kevin Flynn. They had escaped from Clu's forces and recovered Kevin's disc! It was time to head to the Portal and escape to the real world.